No dinosaurs in the park

Dorothy Joan Harris   Sylvie Daigneault

North Winds Press
A Division of Scholastic-TAB Publications Ltd., Richmond Hill, Ontario, Canada

6 5 4 3 2 1   Printed in Hong Kong   0 1 2 3/9

Canadian Cataloguing in Publication Data

Harris, Dorothy Joan, 1931-
    No dinosaurs in the park

Issued also in French under title: Pas de
dinosaures dans le parc.
ISBN 0-590-73210-2

I. Daigneault, Sylvie. II. Title.

PS8565.A77N6 1989   jC813'.54   C89-094567-5
PZ7.H37No 1989

For Nora and for Bob, too.

D.J.H.

For Douglas, Rachel and Benjamin

S.D.

When Grandpa comes to visit we always go to the park. We walk along the path, past the pond and the rock garden, and look at everything. Sometimes I play on the swings while Grandpa pushes me. Sometimes we sit on a bench and Grandpa tells me stories. I almost always ask for stories about dinosaurs.

Today, while we were walking by the pond, Grandpa stopped all of a sudden and said, "Bless my socks! Just look over there — a diplodocus!"

I looked where he was pointing, but all I could see was a big branch floating on the pond.

"Do you see its long, long tail sticking out of the water?" asked Grandpa. "That tail can flick like a whip, you know."

Well, then I saw it. "We'd better hide!" I shouted.

The huge diplodocus flicked its tail, but we hid behind a tree.

"He won't be able to reach us here," Grandpa said.

Just after we escaped from the diplodocus, Grandpa stopped again. "Shhh!" he whispered. "Look over there — a compsognathus. A whole gang of them, in fact."

I looked towards the tall grass. At first I thought it was a bunch of noisy crows.

"A compsognathus is small," Grandpa said, "but it's speedy. I think this gang is hunting for their dinner."

11

"They look hungry," I agreed. "Do you think they'll try to eat us?"

"Probably not," said Grandpa, "but maybe we should scare them away, just in case."

So we roared and we shouted, and they all ran away.

"A compsognathus doesn't like loud noises," said Grandpa.

Suddenly a great winged shape flew overhead.

"Look out! A pterodactyl!" shouted Grandpa. "Red alert! Red alert!"

The other people in the park probably thought it was a Canada goose. But we could see what it really was.

15

We stood very still until it was gone.

"Pterodactyls can't see you if you stand very still," I told Grandpa.

On the way home we walked past the rock garden.

All of a sudden *I* stopped. "Look, Grandpa!" I said. "There's a stegosaurus in those rocks!"

"Well, I'll be hornswoggled," said Grandpa, "so there is! He must be trying to hide. A stegosaurus is a very timid creature, you know."

We coaxed him out with a chocolate ice cream cone. He really liked it, but he was a messy eater and splashed all over my new shirt.

When we got home, I told Mom why my shirt was such a mess. She was a bit cross about it. And she said there are absolutely *no* dinosaurs in the park.

But Grandpa and I know better.